DC COMICS
SUPER HEROES

BATMAN™

AN ORIGIN STORY

Curious Fox

Published in the United Kingdom in 2016 by Curious Fox
an imprint of Capstone Global Library Limited,
264 Banbury Road, Oxford, OX2 7DY
Registered company number: 6695582
www.curious-fox.com

First published by Stone Arch Books
A Capstone Imprint
1710 Roe Crest Drive
North Mankato, MN 56003
www.mycapstone.com

ISBN 978 1 78202 479 8
19 18 17 16 15
10 9 8 7 6 5 4 3 2 1

A full catalogue record for this book is available from the British Library

Contributing artists: Tim Levins, Dan Schoening, Erik Doescher,
Mike DeCarlo, Lee Loughridge and Ethen Beavers
Designed by Hilary Wacholz

Printed and bound in China

DC COMICS™
SUPER HEROES

BATMAN™

AN ORIGIN STORY

WRITTEN BY
JOHN SAZAKALIS

ILLUSTRATED BY
LUCIANO VECCHIO

BATMAN CREATED BY
BOB KANE

Bruce Wayne is a happy boy. He lives in a big mansion in Gotham City.

His parents, Thomas and Martha, love him very much. So does their loyal butler, Alfred Pennyworth.

Bruce has a big imagination. He loves to dress up as his favourite hero.

"En garde!" he shouts.

One evening, Bruce's parents take him to see a film. It's about his favourite action hero.

Young Bruce sits in the cinema. He wears his costume. He eats popcorn.

The film is good!

When the film is over, they leave the cinema.

Bruce and his parents walk through an alley to their car.

The night is dark. A chill is in the air...

A thief appears. He wants Thomas's wallet and Martha's pearl necklace.

Thomas tries to protect his family.

Two shots ring out.

Bruce is suddenly an orphan.

Alfred takes care of Bruce. But
Bruce still feels alone and afraid.

Wayne Manor is big and empty.
The laughter has gone.

Bruce decides that no one else should feel such pain.

He vows to use his life to fight crime. He will spend many years training his body and mind…

Bruce grows up. He leaves Gotham City. He travels to new places. He meets new people.

He learns martial arts.

He soon becomes an expert!

He practises gymnastics. He swims.

He learns to box. Bruce is now

stronger and faster than ever before!

Strength is not enough.

Bruce also trains his mind.

He studies crime scenes. He learns about chemistry.

He reads books on many subjects, from Astronomy to Zoology!

Bruce is ready.

Bruce returns to Gotham City. But he still needs something. A symbol.

He needs a sign to inspire him. He sits down in his study to think.

A bat crashes through the window!

Bruce used to be scared of bats. This is just the sign he needs.

"I will become a bat," Bruce says.
"I will strike fear into the hearts of criminals!"

Bruce gets to work. Soon, Batman is born!

Bruce has a lot of money from his family's fortune.

He uses some of it to build a secret base under Wayne Manor.

He calls this base the Batcave.

Only Alfred knows about the Batcave. He keeps the base in tip-top condition.

Batman creates many new gadgets such as the batarang and grapnel gun. They fit in his Utility Belt.

Batman designs many vehicles. His favourite one is the Batmobile.

It is sleek and armoured. It is faster than a cheetah. It is tougher than a tank!

Batman runs across rooftops. He scans the streets.

He is the silent guardian of Gotham City. He is the Caped Crusader!

Batman protects the people of Gotham City.

Criminals run when Batman arrives.

There isn't a mystery he can't solve.

Batman is the World's Greatest
Detective!

Criminals can't escape when
Batman is on the case.

Stories about Batman spread through the city.

New criminals appear. They want to defeat the Dark Knight.

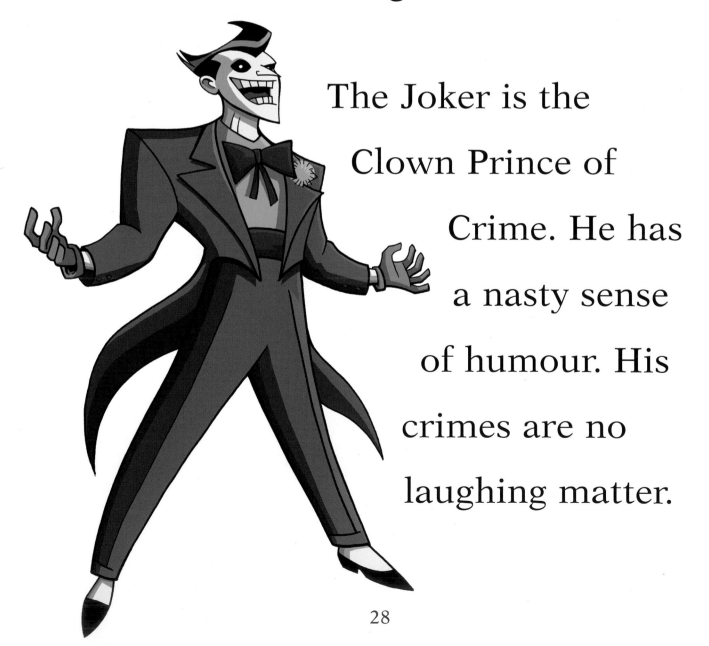

The Joker is the Clown Prince of Crime. He has a nasty sense of humour. His crimes are no laughing matter.

This greedy gangster is the Penguin. He pretends to be a businessman. But he is just a greedy, bird-loving bandit.

Catwoman is a clever cat burglar. She wants to steal all of Gotham's valuable jewels. MEOW!

The Riddler loves to leave clues to his crimes. He wants to beat Batman in a battle of brains.

Mr Freeze has a special suit. He freezes his enemies. He wants the world to be in eternal winter.

Poison Ivy controls plants. She also has a toxic touch. She won't stop until plants rule the world!

Batman has many enemies. But
he is not afraid to face them!

Batman uses his mind. He uses his gadgets. He uses his speed and strength.

Batman does not fight alone. He has a friend in the Police Department.

This police officer trusts Batman. They help each other to fight crime. He is none other than Commissioner Gordon!

Batman also has two young partners.

One is Robin!

The other is Batgirl!

This daring duo know martial arts. They have sharp detective skills. They have trained under Batman's watchful eye. He is their mentor.

Uh-oh! There is trouble in Gotham City.

Commissioner Gordon turns on the Bat-Signal.

The heroes arrive to help!

Together, they can beat any foe.

Batman and his friends keep
Gotham City safe.

They help the people. They fight crime. They right wrongs.

Children need not fear when Batman is near.

Bruce Wayne honours his parents by being a hero.

When danger rises in Gotham City, Batman is there to save the day!

BATMAN

REAL NAME: BRUCE WAYNE
ROLE: CRIME FIGHTER
BASE: GOTHAM CITY

Born into a wealthy, loving family, young Bruce had everything a child could want – until a horrible crime changed his life. Now Bruce protects the innocent from suffering a similar fate.

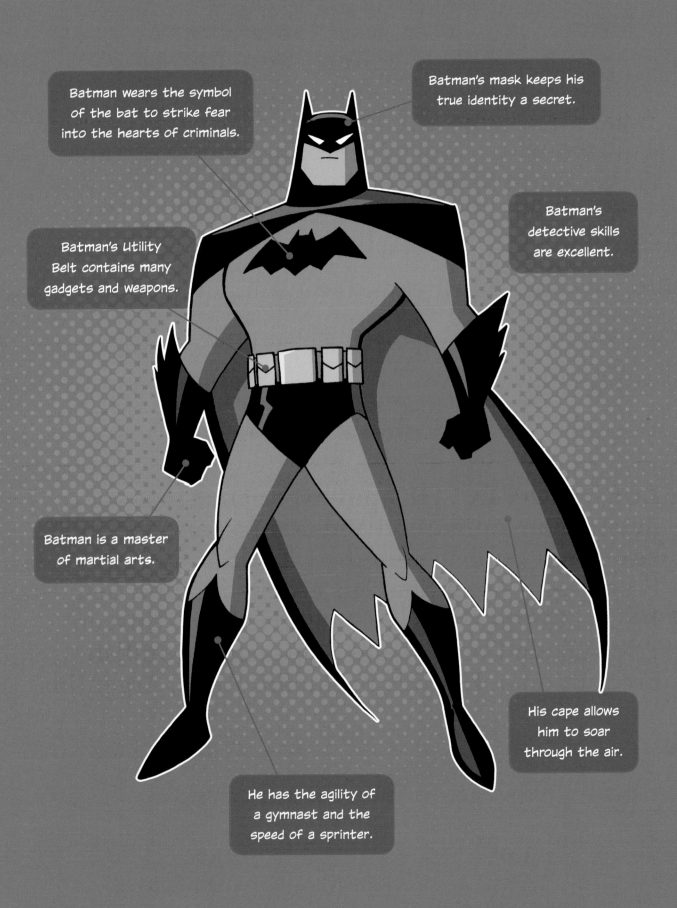

THE AUTHOR

New York Times best-selling author **JOHN SAZAKLIS** enjoys writing children's books about his favourite characters. He has also illustrated Spider-Man books. To him, it's a dream come true! John lives with his beautiful wife in New York, USA.

THE ILLUSTRATOR

LUCIANO VECCHIO has experience in illustration, animation and comics, and his works have been published in the UK, USA, Spain, France and Argentina. His credits include Ben 10 (DC Comics), Cruel Thing (Norma), Unseen Tribe (Zuda Comics) and Sentinels (Drumfish Productions). He lives in Buenos Aires, Argentina.

GLOSSARY

bandit criminal who steals

eternal without end or lasting forever

grapnel device with iron claws attached to a rope, used to drag or hook onto something

guardian someone who watches or protects someone or something

honour show or give great respect

inspire make someone want to do something

mentor someone who teaches or gives help and advice to a less experienced and often younger person

orphan child whose parents are no longer living

sleek smooth and shiny, or having an elegant design

symbol object or image that stands for or represents a certain idea or quality

toxic poisonous

DISCUSSION QUESTIONS

Write down your answers. Refer back to the story for help.

QUESTION 1.

The phrase "En garde!" is French for "On guard!" Based on this illustration, why would Bruce say "On guard!" to his father?

QUESTION 2.

Batman is also known as the World's Greatest Detective. What is Batman doing in this illustration? Write a short story describing what Batman is up to, and what he'll do next.

QUESTION 3.

Batman uses many gadgets to fight crime. Here he is using a batarang. In what ways could Batman use a batarang to fight crime? Come up with as many as you can.

QUESTION 4.

Bruce studied many subjects in his journey to become Batman. What types of skills and knowledge have you learned at school that might come in handy for someone like Batman?

READ THEM ALL!!

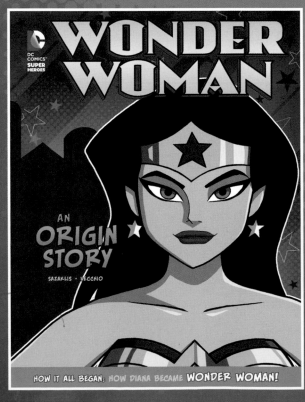

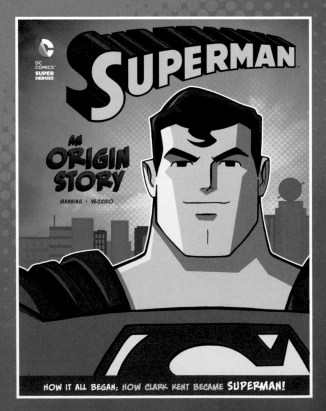